MANABOZHO'S GIFTS

MANABOZHO'S GIFTS
Three Chippewa Tales

Retold by
Jacqueline Dembar Greene

Illustrated by Jennifer Hewitson

Houghton Mifflin Company
Boston 1994

Library of Congress Cataloging-in-Publication Data

Greene, Jacqueline Dembar.
    Manabozho's gifts : three Chippewa tales / by Jacqueline Dembar
Greene ; illustrated by Jennifer Hewitson.
        p.   cm.
    Includes bibliographical references.
    Summary: Three Chippewa legends featuring the mythical hero
Manabozho, who introduces fire and wild rice to his people and saves
the rose from extinction.
    ISBN 0-395-69251-2
    1. Ojibwa Indians—Legends. [1. Ojibwa Indians—Legends.
2. Indians of North America—Legends.]   I. Hewitson, Jennifer, ill.
II. Title.
E99.C6G68   1994   93-41738
[398.2'089973]—dc20   CIP
                        AC

Printed in the United States of America
BP 10 9 8 7 6 5 4 3 2 1

To Mikki and Lani

Contents

Foreword

There are many tales among the native North American people about the adventures of Manabozho. He was believed to be the son of the West Wind and the great-grandson of the Moon. More than a man and less than a god, he had great powers which he used to help his people.

Among Manabozho's greatest powers was the ability to change into any shape he desired. He could become a tree or a stone, an animal or a bird. Once he had transformed himself, he had both the abilities of the shape he assumed and its limits. If he became an eagle, he could soar above the earth, but he couldn't swim. If he became a fish, he could travel beneath the water, but he couldn't breathe on land.

Except for times when he needed the qualities of another creature, Manabozho lived among the people as a man. He had the best qualities of humans, such as kindness, intelligence, and love, but he also suffered as they did from cold and hunger, and sometimes showed foolishness, greed, or selfishness.

The people admired Manabozho's strengths and recognized his weaknesses. He is credited with giving the people their religion and teaching them how to send their prayers to Gitchi Manido, the Great Spirit. He rid the land of evil monsters, taught the people to hunt and fish, gave them the gift of fire and the sustenance of wild rice. Above all, Manabozho taught the people to share the land with animals and plants. He showed them the importance of keeping a balance with the earth, never taking more food than they needed, always being careful to ensure that every life form would continue.

In similar tales told by the Algonquin, the Menominee, the Chippewa (Ojibwa) and other North American peoples, Manabozho is known by many names. He was called Nanabozho, Wenabozho, Winabojo, Manabush, Chiabo, and Hiawatha. But in every case, the stories reflected the love and gratitude the people felt for all that Manabozho did.

MANABOZHO'S GIFTS

How Manabozho Stole Fire

In the time of the First People, long before your strong heart began to beat the rhythm of life, Manabozho made the forest his home.

Manabozho was more than a man. His father was Mudekewis, the great West Wind. His grandmother was Nokomis, daughter of the Moon. Manabozho had mighty powers, and he used them to help his people.

One bitter morning, in the Moon of First Snow, Manabozho found Nokomis shivering in the wigwam. He draped his rabbit fur cloak around her and sat on the cold mats that covered the floor.

"I am too old to fight Kabibonca, the fierce North Wind," Nokomis said. "But I do not want to leave my people and follow the singing birds to the warm lands in the south."

"Everyone suffers in the cold," Manabozho replied "The wigwams are dark and cheerless, and there is little to eat."

Then he remembered something. "Once you told me a tale about Fire, Grandmother. It was a story about a magic flame that glowed with light and warmth. Is there really such a wondrous thing as Fire?"

"Oh, yes," said Nokomis. She rubbed her stiff hands together. "I have heard it can light the darkness and turn ice into water. It is said Fire can make animal meat a nourishing food. But if it is not controlled, Fire is powerful enough to destroy the forest and all that is in it. Long ago Coyote brought Fire from the underworld, but the First People were afraid of it. They gave it into the safekeeping of an old magician who lives on an island far to the west He and his two daughters guard it in their wigwam. In our own time, many have tried to steal it, but all have failed."

Manabozho was angry. "Fire is needed by all the people. I will find the old magician and bring some back."

Nokomis frowned. "It's an impossible task. Stay here where you belong."

But Manabozho was determined. "The Great Spirit will help me," he said.

Nokomis knew she couldn't stop her grandson, and she knew he wasn't like others who had tried to steal Fire "While you are away, I will gather some dry bark and grass. If you are successful, we will need them to nourish

he flame and help it grow." She handed him his rabbit
ur cloak. "Be careful," she warned.

Manabozho stepped into his birch bark canoe. He
wrapped his cloak tightly around him and placed his hands
on the edges of the boat.

"Westward, westward," he commanded, and it glided swiftly and silently across the water.

Hours passed and the sun fell lower in the sky before Manabozho reached a barren, windswept island. He hid his canoe among the rushes and kept watch. As the shadows lengthened, two strong young women walked toward the shore holding empty jugs. Their voices carried across the clear air.

"Father wants to eat hot soup tonight," said the Tall Sister. "We will need plenty of water." Her hair fell loosely over her shoulders as she looked for an opening in the thin ice close to shore.

Manabozho was certain these were the daughters of the old magician. Without Fire, no one could prepare hot food. He pulled his cloak over his head and held it tightly around him.

"Once as a man," he chanted, "now as a rabbit. A rabbit, a rabbit will I be." His fingers curled up into furry paws. His eyes grew narrow and whiskers sprouted from his cheeks. His fur cloak became his rabbit skin, right down to the round fluffy tail.

Just as the sisters approached the edge of the lake, Manabozho hopped across and jumped into a hole in the ice. How cold the water was! His fur was soaked. It pulled him under the water and he struggled for breath.

"Poor little rabbit," said Tall Sister. She scooped Manabozho up in her jug. "He's shivering. Let's bring him into

4

the wigwam and let him dry off by the fire."

"Father will be angry," argued the other sister, whose hair was pulled back in a thick braid. "Leave him here."

Manabozho looked sadly at the young woman who held him. His teeth chattered. "Poor cold rabbit," she crooned, and carried him to the wigwam.

As soon as they entered, Manabozho felt a warmth that enveloped him like the summer sun. The wigwam was bright, and he looked around with his sharp rabbit eyes.

The old magician was asleep on a bearskin blanket. His hair was the color of slate, and it spread around his head in a tangled mass. He snored loudly.

Thick Braid filled an earthen pot with water. She and Tall Sister cut up potatoes and beans and sweet-smelling herbs and added them to the pot. Then they placed it over the hot flames. So this was how to make soup, Manabozho thought. He would remember to tell Nokomis. Manabozho hopped closer to the fire. The water had been colder than he expected and he was shaking all over.

The old man stirred and grumbled. He squinted toward his daughters. "What's wrong?" he demanded. "I sense danger."

"It's nothing, Father," said Tall Sister. "It's just a rabbit I saved from drowning in the lake. I put him near the fire to dry off."

The magician pushed his hair from his eyes and looked at the bedraggled animal suspiciously. "I have heard that

Manabozho can change himself into any shape he desires. He can be a tree or a bird, a rock or a cloud. Perhaps he has changed himself into a rabbit and has come to steal Fire from us."

Tall Sister laughed, and the sound was like broken ice tinkling on a stone. "Go back to sleep, Father. It's just a harmless rabbit."

"Then use his meat for a stew," the old man grumbled. "And save his fur to line my moccasins. My feet are cold in this weather." He rolled over and soon was snoring again.

Manabozho watched carefully and moved his ears to pick up any sign of danger. But the magician's daughters did not seem as if they were about to follow their father's orders.

He warmed his tail near the orange flames and thought of what he should do. With the power of Fire, his people could all keep warm. Their wigwams would be as bright as sunshine, even on a dark winter night. They could hunt animals in the snow and cook fresh meat.

Tall Sister and Thick Braid stirred the pot of soup that hung over the fire and busied themselves at other tasks. Now Manabozho's fur was dry and he felt warm again.

"I think Father is right," said Thick Braid. "Perhaps the Great Spirit has sent this rabbit to keep us from hunger. We should add his meat to the pot and make a good stew."

"I saved him from the river," said Tall Sister, "and I will not see him harmed."

Manabozho knew he must act quickly. While the women argued, he grasped a hot ember in his paw, dropped it onto his back and leaped toward the door flap.

"He's stealing our Fire!" shouted the magician. Manabozho didn't know how the old man had sensed what was happening, since he had seemed to be asleep.

"Catch him!" shouted Thick Braid. She ran after Manabozho and Tall Sister followed.

The magician jumped from his bed. His eyes flashed red. "Foolish daughters! I warned you about Manabozho. Catch him before he gives our precious Fire to all the earth people!"

Manabozho dashed out of the wigwam, but the sisters were right behind him. He thought they must be strong and powerful to run as fast as a rabbit.

When he came to the icy lake, he hopped lightly across until he came to his canoe. The magician's daughters were too big and heavy to cross the thin ice. They stood on the shore and threw a hail of stones at Manabozho. Although many of the stones hit him, they didn't hurt as much as the hot ember that burned fiercely into his back.

Manabozho leaped into his canoe and held onto the sides with his paws. "Homeward, homeward," he commanded, and the boat raced across the cold waters.

Now the stones fell into the water with loud splashes, and the magician's daughters looked smaller and smaller as Manabozho sped away.

When he reached the shores of his home, dawn was breaking over the forest. The glowing ember burned into his skin.

"Grandmother!" he shouted. "I've brought Fire! Bring the bark and grasses!" He hopped into the wigwam and dropped the ember onto the dry tinder that Nokomis had prepared. There was a spark and a stream of smoke, and then an orange glow. Nokomis placed small sticks onto the fire until it grew to life.

But Manabozho could not enjoy his success. His back still burned painfully. He rolled on the cold dirt floor. Nokomis looked at him and laughed. "You don't have to stay a rabbit," she reminded him.

Manabozho had forgotten his own powers. "Once as a rabbit, now as a man," he sang. "A man, a man will I be." His fur fell away in one piece, leaving his cloak crumpled at his feet. He again stood before Nokomis as a human. He rubbed his strong hands together and was relieved to find that his back was not burning any longer. As he warmed himself by the fire, he forgot the pain his adventure had caused and thought only of the gift he had brought for his people.

But whenever he put on his rabbit fur cloak, there was one lasting reminder. At the very bottom, just above the tail, there was a black, singed patch of fur that stood out as a mark of courage for all to see.

How Manabozho Found Rice

In the Moon of Ripe Berries, Manabozho walked through the village. Women and children came in from the forest carrying baskets of plump blueberries, sweet raspberries, and tart cranberries, bursting with juice. They spread the ripe fruit on woven mats to dry under the hot sun.

Nokomis squatted on the grass, guarding the fruit from the hungry ravens and blue jays that shrieked and cackled in the trees. Whenever the birds flew too close to the berries, she flapped a piece of deer skin to scare them away.

"Father Sun favors us with his hot breath," said Manabozho. "We will have a great store of fruit when Kabibonca, the fierce North Wind, blows against the wigwam."

Nokomis nodded. "I'll save as many baskets of berries

as I can. I will make pemmican cakes, too. They will be good."

Manabozho's mouth watered at the thought of his grandmother's pemmican cakes. She mixed berries with dried meat and plenty of bear fat, as did all the women, but she added special herbs that made hers the tastiest.

"And I gathered a store of cherry twigs and raspberry leaves that we can brew into hot drinks," Nokomis added. "Having fire to warm our food makes it easier to get through the cold days."

Still, Manabozho knew there was never enough food to last until the people returned to the fishing grounds in the spring Moon of Flowers. He thought of the long winters when there was little to eat. Many of the animals slept through the cold moons. They didn't need to eat every day. But his people did.

Manabozho made up his mind. There must be a way to save more food. There had to be something that would nourish the people and would not spoil during the many days that it must be stored. He tied his medicine bag around his waist.

"I am going into the forest, Grandmother. I will fast and pray to Gitchi Manido, the Great Spirit. Perhaps he will send me a vision that will give me the power to help my people through the winter."

As Manabozho walked through the forest, he greeted all the wood people. He chatted with the birds and snakes,

rabbits and deer, for he had learned their language when he was still a child.

The day drew to a close, and he rested on the edge of the Great Water. He saw a beaver lodge that was built across the mouth of a quick-running stream.

"Where are you going?" asked Beaver. "You have traveled far from your village."

"I, too, will build a lodge here," Manabozho said. "I will stay and hope the spirits will send me a dream or a vision so I can help my people. I must find something that will keep us from going hungry during the long winters."

Beaver and his family gnawed down some nearby saplings, and Manabozho set them firmly into the ground, bending them into a round frame. Then he covered them with strips of birch bark. He dug a small pit in the center of the new wigwam, filled it with twigs and grass, and rubbed two sticks together until he had started a small fire. Now that the people had mastered its use, their lives were easier. Manabozho was pleased with his gift of Fire, but now his people needed more.

He took a small pinch of tobacco from his medicine pouch and dropped it onto the flames. A sweet-smelling smoke wafted into the air and curled through the opening in the wigwam roof.

"Great Spirit," he prayed, "you have given me many powers. You have heard my people's prayers and allowed me to help them. Take this sacred tobacco into your home in the sky and hear me. Show me the way to provide more food for my people, so they will not suffer hunger when the North Wind howls and snow covers the earth."

For three days, Manabozho watched the waves chase each other upon the water. He marked the setting of the fiery orange sun and the rising of the ghost-white moon. He drank water from the clear lake, but ate no food. All day he prayed to Gitchi Manido, but he saw no vision, and at night when he slept, he had no dreams.

On the fourth day, Manabozho was tired and weak, but he would not end his fasting. He smothered the fire carefully with handfuls of sand and rolled up the bark sheets that covered his small wigwam.

To the Beaver he said, "Take these poles and use them to strengthen your lodge. I won't forget the help you have given me."

"Are you going home?" asked Beaver. "Is there no answer to your vision quest?"

Manabozho was tired, but he was not ready to give up. "I shall walk along the shore and think. Perhaps the spirits don't wish to visit me here. During the day, I will let the sun shine upon my back, and at night the stars will see my face. Then, maybe, Gitchi Manido will find me."

He wandered all day and into the night. His stomach ached with hunger and his feet felt heavy. Then, in the moonlight, he saw a group of dancers weaving and bending. He couldn't hear their drums, but felt their rhythm. In spite of his weariness, he stepped forward.

"May I join your dance?"

But there was no answer. The dancers swayed gracefully

and their feathered headdresses rippled in the night breeze. Again he addressed them.

"Can a weary traveler join your dance?"

Still, the dancers would not stop. Ignoring their rudeness, he stepped among them, lifting his feet and swaying with the wind. He tossed his long, straight hair in imitation of their waving headdresses.

Manabozho felt his weariness fly from him. His feet were light again and his heart leaped with each joyful step. All night he moved with the silent dancers until he fell, exhausted, upon the sand and slept.

The sun awoke him the next morning. He opened his eyes, remembering the festive night. But where were the dancers now? He stood and looked around. He was alone on the bank of a quiet bay, surrounded by graceful reeds bending under the morning dew.

Then Manabozho realized he had been tricked. The silent dancers were the reeds that swayed at the water's edge. The feathered headdresses that seemed to be rippling in the breeze were the tasseled plumes that crowned each one.

"I have been a fool," he scolded himself, "thinking the reeds were dancers. No wonder they didn't answer me when I asked if I might join them!"

But then Manabozho thought of his quest. Perhaps the spirits wanted him to stay in this place. Maybe the vision of the dancing reeds was meant to stop his wandering.

Then he noticed something he had never seen before. In the bay, where the shallow water deepened, grew tall plants that towered above all others.

He took off his moccasins and waded in. The plants loomed above him, each one nearly as tall as a birch tree. They bore broad, shimmering leaves and had sprays of needlelike grains sprouting from their stems.

Manabozho was struck by their beauty. Why had he never seen such graceful plants before?

"I must show these to Nokomis," he said aloud. "Perhaps she will know what they are called."

The morning breeze rustled through the leaves and the plants seemed to whisper to Manabozho. He listened, trying to understand their meaning.

"Manomin they call us," murmured the plants. "Manomin, the Good Berry." Bending the tall plant down, Manabozho shook some of the grains into his hand.

"Sometimes they eat us," said Manomin.

A flock of ducks landed on the water and began eating the seeds that had fallen from the plants. Manabozho collected handfuls of grain and ate them. His hunger was satisfied and the seeds did not make him ill.

"Gitchi Manido has sent an answer to my prayers," he told the plant. "You will give your grain to feed my people."

Manabozho traveled back to the village, remembering to stop along the way to retrieve the birch bark he had saved from his small wigwam. He and Nokomis returned

together to the quiet bay. They set up camp and protected the wondrous plants from the hungry birds until the grain was all ripened. Then they went out in Manabozho's canoe and shook the grains into the boat until it was filled.

They were careful to leave enough seeds so that the ducks and birds would not go hungry, and new plants would spring up in the muddy shallows.

The people learned to harvest manomin, and parch it over the fire so it could be stored in birch bark baskets during the long winters. They ate it dry. They cooked it in soups and stews. They boiled it into a thick mixture that warmed them on cold mornings.

Every summer, the people set up camps along the rivers and streams and bays where the magnificent manomin, which we call wild rice, grew to towering heights. They collected it and prepared it so that no one would go hungry when Kabibonca blew against the wigwam and the earth was covered with a cold blanket of snow.

And everywhere that Manabozho traveled, he scattered the grains along the quiet streams so that no matter where his people traveled they would not go hungry again.

How Manabozho Saved the Rose

At the end of summer, in the month of the Harvest Moon, Manabozho saw the Moon glowing ghostly white in the afternoon sky.

"Nokomis!" he called. "The Moon is out of place, shining so brightly in the day. What does it mean?"

His grandmother looked up from the moccasins she was embroidering with hollow porcupine quills. "My mother, the Moon, is sending us a warning. Something is not the way it should be."

"I will talk to my brothers, the wood people," Manabozho said, "and see what they can tell me."

Manabozho walked until he came to a clearing in the forest. A family of bears sprawled on the ground. They looked thin and tired.

29

"Greetings," he said. "Why is it that you rest during the day? You should be hunting for food to fatten yourselves for the long winter sleep."

The cubs stared quietly at Manabozho, instead of tumbling and romping at his feet as they usually did. Mother Bear sat up with great effort. "It's the bees," she complained. "They are not making enough honey to share with us. What little we have found is thin and less sweet than it used to be."

Manabozho wondered if the lack of honey had anything to do with the Moon's warning. "Let's find the bees. Perhaps they can tell us what is wrong."

They walked slowly through the woods and into a wide meadow dotted with wildflowers. A swarm of bees hovered in the air.

"Do you see?" Father Bear growled. "The bees are lazy. They aren't making enough honey!"

"Don't accuse us!" said the bees. They buzzed close to the bear's tender nose. "There isn't enough sweet nectar to feed us." Two hummingbirds flew toward them.

"We, too, are starving," they said. Manabozho could see how thin their bodies were beneath their glossy feathers.

Other wood people began to gather around Manabozho. There were foxes and deer, rabbits and woodchucks, blue jays, squirrels, snakes and beaver, all asking what was wrong.

"The Moon is sending us a message," he said, pointing

to the sky. "Something is not as it should be. Look around you. Do you see what is missing?"

The animals looked across the meadow and at once all seemed to understand. "It's the roses!" they answered. "There are no roses!"

The deer looked ashamed. "We have sometimes trampled them," a tall buck confessed, "but they were always so plentiful, it was hard not to find one underfoot."

"We noticed there weren't as many roses the past few summers," admitted a woodchuck, "but as with all things, some years there are plenty, and some years there are few. We were certain the roses would return."

"I, too, saw that the roses were disappearing," cackled the blue jay. "I used to admire their brilliant colors when I flew across the meadows. But this year I didn't see a single one."

Manabozho was disappointed with the wood people. "You all knew that the roses were in trouble, but none of you tried to help."

The bees grew quiet. The deer hung their heads. The hummingbirds' wings drooped.

The bears spoke up. "We must all set out and search for the roses. And we must hope they haven't all died."

The snakes slithered through the grasses and slid over rocks. Bears clambered through the forest and sniffed the air for the roses' sweet fragrance. Squirrels jumped across the treetops and looked far across the meadows.

Manabozho was certain there were no roses nearby. He gazed up at the sky and spoke to Gitchi Manido, "Far must I fly, and fast. A hummingbird, a hummingbird I must be." In the blink of an eye, Manabozho's body became small. His hair turned to rainbow-colored feathers that shimmered in the sunlight. His arms became a blur of beating wings. He rose above the wood people, hovered for a moment, and then soared away, over the fields and across the horizon, looking for just one spot of bright color.

Nokomis gathered the earth people, and they, too, roamed the forests and fields in search of the rose. For three days, the animals and the people searched. But each day they returned to their meeting place without success.

On the fourth day, a weary Manabozho landed in the center of the group. In his beak he held a wilted plant bearing one pale, yellow rose.

The medicine man and medicine woman dug a deep hole for the wilted rose. They filled it with rich soil and set the roots down firmly. They watered it and chanted songs of life. The wood people and the earth people watched and waited.

The rose began to revive and spoke in a faint whisper. All strained to hear. "I am the last of my family. Every year you stepped on us carelessly. You watched us disappear and thought it didn't matter. But worst of all were the rabbits." The limp rose bent toward the silent rabbits.

"You chewed our blossoms without leaving any seeds to sow new plants."

All eyes turned to the rabbits. Everyone saw that, unlike all the other animals, the rabbits were plump and healthy.

"It's your fault," they shouted. The bears and wolves seized the rabbits by their ears and shook them hard. Their ears stretched and stretched. The beaver swatted them with their flat tails and split their lips.

Manabozho flew into the group. "Once as a bird, now as a man," he chanted. "A man, a man I must be." His feathers turned back into long, thick hair. His wings became long arms with strong fingers. His body grew back into that of a man.

Manabozho stepped among the fighting animals and raised his hand. His great shadow fell across the group. At once they stopped, afraid of his anger.

"The rabbits have done great harm," he said, "and for that reason let them always wear the mark of their shame. From this time on, their ears will flop and their mouths will be split." Then he pointed to every creature around him.

"But we are all to blame. We must remember that plants can live very well without us. But without them, neither the wood people nor the earth people can live."

Manabozho looked up at the sky, and everyone followed his gaze. The Moon had faded and the sun alone shone on the gathering.

Now Manabozho bent down to the rose and touched its stem. "From now on you will be protected. Any creature who carelessly tramples you or tries to eat your blooms will remember your sting." All along the rose's stem, sharp thorns sprang out.

Manabozho shooed the animals and earth people off, but the bees and the hummingbirds still remain close by the rose, and watch it year after year to be sure it survives.

Notes

Research into tales and myths of the Chippewa people for this book drew upon all the sources listed in the following bibliography, many of which contain variations of similar tales. The name Manabozho was chosen over others because it stems from the Algonquin people, to which the Chippewa are related, especially in language. In addition, it is considered the primary spelling in the Archaeological Institute of America's reference series, *Mythology of All Races*.

Dorothy Reid's *Tales of Manabozho* and Thomas B. Leekley's *The World of Manabozho* became the main sources for my retelling of "How Manabozho Stole Fire." In this story, I have changed the season to emphasize life without fire. I used dramatic fiction to create Manabozho's magical words to transform his shape and command his canoe, although reference to his order, "Westward, westward," is found in *Manabozho, The Indian's Story of Hiawatha* by Alden Deming. The primary source for "How Manabozho Found Rice" is one of the variations related in Sonia Bleeker's

The Chippewa Indians. It is combined here with the legend of Manabozho's encounter with the reed dancers related in Dorothy M. Brown's report on "Manabush—Menomini Tales." The third tale in this volume, "How Manabozho Saved the Rose," is based upon information in Basil Johnston's *Ojibway Heritage* and Egerton Young's *Algonquin Indian Tales.* My modifications to the story include having Manabozho change himself into a hummingbird, in keeping with his traditional powers.

For Further Reading

Bleeker, Sonia. *The Chippewa Indians.* New York: William Morrow and Co., 1955.

Greene, Jacqueline Dembar. *The Chippewa.* New York: Franklin Watts, 1993.

Reqquinti, Gordon. *The Sacred Harvest.* Minneapolis: Lerner Publications, 1992.

Stan, Susan. *The Ojibwe.* Florida: Rourke Publications, 1989.

Bibliography

Barnouw, Victor. *Wisconsin Chippewa Myths and Tales.* Madison, WI: University of Wisconsin Press, 1977.

Bleeker, Sonia. *The Chippewa Indians.* New York: William Morrow and Co., 1955.

Coatsworth, Emerson and David Coatsworth. *The Adventures of Nanabush: Ojibway Indian Stories.* New York: Atheneum, 1980.

Deming, Alden O. *Manabozho, The Indian's Story of Hiawatha.* Philadelphia: F. A. Davis Co., 1938.

Johnston, Basil. *Ojibway Heritage.* New York: Columbia University Press, 1976.

Leekley, Thomas B. *The World of Manabozho.* New York: Vanguard Press, 1965.

MacCulloch, Canon John Arnott. *Mythology of All Races.* Boston: Plimpton Press, 1932.

Morriseau, Norval. *Legends of My People, The Great Ojibway.* Toronto: Ryerson Press, 1965.

Reid, Dorothy M. *Tales of Manabozho.* New York: Henry Z. Walck, Inc., 1963.

Schoolcraft, Henry. *Legends of the American Indians.* New York: Crescent Book, n.d.

Thompson, Stith. *Tales of the North American Indians.* Bloomington: Indiana University Press, 1967.

Warren, Maude Radford. *Manabozho, The Great White Rabbit.* New York: Rand McNally, 1920.

Young, Egerton. *Algonquin Indian Tales.* New York: Fleming Revell Co., 1903.